Published in the United States by Grolier
Books, a division of Grolier Enterprises, Inc.

First American Edition.

ISBN: 0-7172-8353-4

The animals came from far and near across the dusty African plain. They came on padding paws and pounding hooves and flapping wings.

Each beast, from the tiniest ant to the largest elephant, made its way to Pride Rock. For that was the home of the Lion King, and this was a special day in the Pride Lands.

Today Simba, the first-born cub of King Mufasa and Queen Sarabi, would join the great Circle of Life.

The animals took their places and bowed to King Mufasa. Then Rafiki, the wise baboon, stood at the edge of Pride Rock and held up the little cub for all to see.

A great cry rose from all the animals. The elephants trumpeted, the zebras whinnied, and the
birds sang for joy at the sight of Simba, the
future lion king.

But one animal did not join in the joyous ceremony. Scar, the King's jealous brother, stayed in
his den.

Later, Scar just laughed when the King's advisor, Zazu the hornbill, criticized him. Then the evil lion popped the bird into his mouth. Scar would have eaten Zazu if Mufasa hadn't come along just in time.

Zazu wiped his feathers off and scolded, "As the King's brother, you should have been first in line at Simba's ceremony."

Scar's green eyes gleamed. "I was first in line, until the little hairball was born."

"That hairball is my son, and your future king," Mufasa growled.

Scar slinked away.

"Don't turn your back on me!" Mufasa warned.

Scar looked back over his shoulder. His eyes narrowed. "Perhaps *you* shouldn't turn your back on *me*."

Simba grew quickly. One morning Mufasa took his son to the top of Pride Rock and told him, "The Circle of Life never stops turning. One day the sun will set on my time as ruler and rise with you as king. Then everything the light touches will be yours."

"What about that shadowy place?" Simba asked.

Mufasa declared, "You must never go there."

Suddenly Zazu swooped down and squawked, "Hyenas in the Pride Lands!"

Mufasa frowned. "Zazu, take Simba home."

"Aw, Dad, can't I come?" Simba whined.

Mufasa shook his mighty mane. Fighting savage hyenas was no job for a cub.

Later, Simba asked his Uncle Scar about the shadowy place.

An evil plan formed in Scar's mind. "Only the bravest lions go to the elephant graveyard," Scar told him. He knew the foolish cub would go there just to prove his bravery.

Scar was right. Simba couldn't wait to go to
the elephant graveyard with his best friend,
Nala. But how could they go with Zazu watching
every move they made?

"We've got to ditch the dodo," Simba whispered.

Nala giggled and agreed. Soon the two friends
found a way to escape their feathered baby-sitter.

Before long the young lions had reached the
dark, mysterious place beyond the borders of the
Pride Lands. Giant bones poked out of the ground.

"It's kind of scary," Nala whispered.

"Let's check it out," Simba said. "I laugh in the
face of danger. Ha-ha-ha!"

"Hee-hee-hee!" cackled three mean hyenas,
Shenzi, Banzai, and Ed.

"Look, boys! A king fit for a meal," Shenzi
snickered.

The cubs ran
but soon found
themselves
cornered.
Simba stepped
bravely in
front of Nala
and tried to
roar. "Rrr . . .
rrr . . . rrr . . ."

The hyenas laughed and jeered.
Simba opened his mouth to try again. This
time the elephant bones rattled with a thunderous
ROAR!

The hyenas were confused. And so was Simba, until Mufasa sprang into view. The mighty lion chased away the hyenas. Zazu had seen the cubs in trouble and flown for help.

Mufasa told Zazu to take Nala home. Then he scolded Simba for disobeying him.

"Aw, Dad. I was just trying to be brave, like you," Simba explained.

Mufasa sighed. "Being brave doesn't mean you go looking for trouble, Simba. A good king is wise as well as brave."

Simba suddenly felt very small. "We'll always be together. Right, Dad?"

Mufasa looked up at the starry sky and said, "The great kings of the past look down on us from those stars. So whenever you feel alone, just remember that those kings will always be there to guide you . . . and so will I."

Later, Scar met with the hungry hyenas. "I practically gave those cubs to you," he complained.

"They weren't exactly alone," Shenzi whined.

But Scar had another plan that would allow him to become king. "Stick with me, and you'll never go hungry again," he promised.

The hyenas danced and cheered.

The next morning Scar took Simba to the bottom of a rocky canyon. "Now wait here," he ordered. "Your father has a big surprise for you."

"Will I like the surprise?" Simba asked.

Scar smiled slyly. "Oh, it's to die for," he said as he walked away. Then he gave a signal to the hyenas waiting on the canyon ridge.

The hyenas knew what to do. They chased a huge herd of wildebeests down the canyon.

Simba felt the earth shake. He heard the clattering of thousands of hooves. Then he saw the wildebeests heading straight for him!

Simba managed to climb a dead tree and cling to a branch. "Help!" he shouted.

Help was on its way, for Scar had found his brother. "Mufasa! Simba's trapped in a stampede!" Scar cried.

Just as Scar had planned, Mufasa rushed to
Simba's rescue. He lifted his son to safety, but
then fell under the rushing tide of hooves.

"Dad!" Simba shouted. He couldn't see any-
thing through the huge dust cloud.

Mufasa tried to pull himself up the steep rocks.
From above, Scar watched his brother struggle.

"Help me! Brother, help me," Mufasa pleaded.

Scar reached for Mufasa's paws. He pulled his
brother close and whispered, "Long live the king!"

Then Scar let go and watched Mufasa tumble
down the steep slope.

When the stampede was over, Simba found his father lying lifeless in the dust. "Noooo!" Simba wailed.

Scar came to the sobbing cub's side. "What have you done?" he accused.

"There were wildebeests everywhere . . . he tried to save me . . . it was an accident," Simba said in a rush. "I didn't mean to . . ."

"Of course not. But if it weren't for you, he'd still be alive. What will your mother think?" Scar demanded.

Simba looked stricken. "What should I do?"

"Run away," Scar advised. "Run away, and never come back."

Scar watched Simba run. Then he sent the hyenas after him.

The hyenas chased Simba to the border of the Pride Lands. The cub dived into a thicket of thorns at the edge of a great desert. The hyenas looked at the sharp thorns, then at the desert.

"The cub won't last a day out there," Shenzi declared.

Simba ran until he could run no more. The thirsty cub collapsed on the sand. Vultures circled him hungrily.

But Timon the meerkat and his fat friend, Pumbaa the warthog, chased away the vultures. Simba woke up in their jungle home.

"Where are you from?" Timon asked.

Simba sighed. "It doesn't matter. I can't go back."

"What did you do, kid?" Pumbaa wondered.

"Something terrible," Simba replied.

Timon shrugged. "Who cares? You've got to put the past behind you. Hakuna Matata!"

"What?" Simba asked.

"Ha-ku-na Ma-ta-ta," Timon repeated. "It means no worries. That's the motto we live by. And here's what we live on." Timon showed Simba a wiggly insect.

Simba watched
Pumbaa eat a grub.
"Slimy, but
satisfying!" the
warthog said with
a burp.
Simba frowned, but
he ate the big grub.

Then the cub smiled and said,
"Hakuna Matata!"

In the months that followed, Simba ate many,
many grubs and grew into a full-sized lion. Most
of the time, he was happy with his friends Timon
and Pumbaa. Yet he missed his mother and
often thought of his father.

One night, as they gazed up at the stars,
Simba remembered what his father had told
him. He wondered if the great kings of the past
really were looking down from those stars.
Simba felt very alone.

The next day Simba heard Timon scream! The young lion raced to the rescue. A hungry lioness was about to pounce on Pumbaa, who was stuck under a log. Timon bravely was trying to protect him. Simba gave a mighty roar and leaped at the lioness.

But just as they began to fight, Simba recognized his old friend. "Nala!" he gasped in disbelief.

The lioness looked deep into the eyes of the handsome young lion and whispered, "Simba? Scar told us you were dead."

Nala told Simba how terrible things were now that King Scar and his hyenas ruled the Pride Lands. There was no food or water, and many of the animals had fled. "But you can come back and become king. Then everything will be right again," Nala said.

"I'm no king," Simba said angrily.

But that night Rafiki the baboon came to Simba and promised to bring him to his father. When Simba looked up at the stars, he heard a familiar voice.

"Simba," his father asked, "have you forgotten me?"

Simba gasped. "No! How could I . . ."

"You have forgotten who you are, and so have forgotten me," the ghostly voice continued. "Look inside yourself, Simba. You are more than what you have become. You must take your place in the Circle of Life!"

Simba knew his father was right. His friends returned with him to the Pride Lands.

Back at Pride Rock, King Scar was angry with Sarabi for not finding food. Suddenly Scar heard a great ROAR! He couldn't believe his eyes. "Mufasa? It can't be. You're dead."

But Sarabi recognized her son. "Simba," she said softly.

"I've come to take my place as king!" Simba roared.

But Scar would not back down so easily.

Simba leaped at Scar, but the villain slipped
away. Instead, the hyenas rushed at Simba. Pride
Rock echoed with their hideous laughter as the
hyenas forced Simba to the edge of a cliff.

Scar walked up to
the exhausted young
lion. "Your daddy
isn't here to save you
this time," Scar taunt-
ed. Then he pushed
Simba off the cliff!

Simba's claws
scrambled for a hold
on the steep slope.

"This looks famil-
iar," Scar sneered.
"Oh, yes, I remember.
It's just the way your
father looked before I
killed him."

At last Simba knew the truth! With a mighty roar, he leaped at Scar.

Meanwhile Timon, Pumbaa, and the lionesses had chased the hyenas off Pride Rock. When Simba sent Scar flying over the cliff, the villain landed in the mob of hungry hyenas.

"Hee-hee-hee," they cackled cruelly. Finally they had a meal fit for a king — or a king fit for a meal!

Simba thanked his friends. Then he walked to
the top of Pride Rock. His roar echoed through
the Pride Lands. The rightful king had taken his
throne.

The plains were soon lush and green again.
The animals returned, and the hunting was good
once more.

Simba knew that a king must have a queen.
So, of course, he chose the beautiful Nala.

Before long, the animals again came
from far and near across the dusty
African plain. This time, they came to greet the
first-born cub of King Simba and Queen Nala.

Wise old Rafiki stood at the edge of Pride Rock
and held up the cub for all to see. The elephants
trumpeted and the zebras whinnied for joy as the
future lion king joined the great Circle of Life.